Pilot Ollie & Pilot Polly's
Amazing Adventures

www. planecharacters.com

Plane Characters Ltd ©

Flag Hunt!
See if you can find all the Spanish flags.

It is a lovely morning when Pilot Polly wakes up. She does a massive YAAWWNNN and has a big stretch!

It is time to go to work again. "I wonder where my travels will take me today?" she thinks.

After a quick shower, Pilot Polly puts on her uniform. She looks very smart in her uniform, especially when she wears her hat.

She looks in the mirror to see if it is straight and then sets off for work.

When she arrives at the airport, Pilot Polly bumps into Chris Controller who is filling the flight folder with the maps for today's flight.

"Good Morning Chris Controller," says Pilot Polly. "It's a lovely day."

"Good Morning Pilot Polly," says Chris Controller. "Shall we sit down and have a look at the maps for todays flight?"

The two of them spread the big map out on the table. "Today," says Chris Controller, "you are going to fly to Madrid in Spain."

"Fantástico!" says Pilot Polly, which means fantastic in Spanish. Pilot Polly was born in Spain and moved to London when she was nine years old.

She can speak English and Spanish and loves going back to Spain.

Woody Weatherman has already put some weather maps in to the flight folder.

Pilot Polly studies them carefully. Can you see what the weather is going to be like?

Today the weather is going to be a bit cloudy, a bit sunny and very hot!

Pilot Polly puts the maps and weather charts into her flight bag and heads out to the plane where the crew are already waiting.

"Hello Molly, hello Mike, hello Megan," she says as she gets onboard the plane.

The flight is full today.

The passengers catch a bus from the airport terminal to the plane and once they are all onboard Chris Controller clears Pilot Polly to start the big jet engines.

"**Chocks Away!**" says Pilot Polly and they're on their way to Spain.

In the flight deck there is a lever that looks like a stick with a wheel on the end.

It's used to move the plane's wheels up and down. As soon as the plane flies into the air, Pilot Polly reaches forward from her seat and lifts the lever up.

The wheels go up and are stored safely away until they are needed for landing.

The flight to Spain takes about two hours. During the flight the cabin crew Megan, Molly and Mike serve drinks and snacks to the passengers.

What drink would you have?

As the sky below the plane is clear the views out of the windows are stunning.

As the plane passes over some mountains, Pilot Polly talks to the passengers.

"Hello everyone," she says, "we are flying at 35,000 feet and our speed is 500 miles an hour. If you look out the windows you will see some amazing snow covered mountains."

Pilot Polly programmes the plane's computers with the weather in Spain.

As they come in to land, she reaches forward, pushes the wheel lever down and the wheels go down ready for landing.

Once all the passengers are off the plane Pilot Polly and the crew set off to explore Madrid.

As the crew walk along the streets Pilot Polly can hear the sound of a guitar playing and people clapping.

They follow the music around a corner and see three Flamenco dancers performing for a small crowd.

The dancing is fast and exciting and the crew stand and watch the ladies dresses swishing around as they play Castanets with their fingers.

Castanets are two wooden shells held together by a string. Pushing the shells together with your fingers makes a clackety-clack sound.

It is lunchtime and Mike says he is hungry.

There is a taverna on the street corner right by the flamenco dancers where the crew can sit outside, watch the dancing and have some lunch.

So that's what they do.

Pilot Polly wants something traditionally Spanish for her lunch. She looks at the menu and sees that they serve Paella. She loves Paella.

When the waiter brings it out, it is a large bowl, bubbling hot, full of lovely fish and rice.

"Gracias," (gra-thee-as) says Pilot Polly, which means thank you in Spanish.

The crew are all full up after their amazing lunch. They still have a couple of hours to go before the flight home so they set off to explore some more.

Walking around they stumble across a huge building. It is absolutely massive.

"That's the Royal Palace," says Megan. She had been reading a guide book on Madrid during lunch.

"It's the biggest royal palace in Western Europe." The crew stand and marvel at the palace. Mike takes some photos.

Can you see the huge Spanish flag?

The clouds have cleared away, the sun is blazing and the crew are getting hot as they wander the streets back to the airport.

"If you see a shop," says Pilot Polly, "I'll pop in and buy some nice cold water."

"There's a shop," says Mike, so they wander in.

The shop keeper can see that the crew are hot from walking around in the sun. She reaches under the counter and pulls out a beautiful paper fan.

"Spain is famous for its beautiful paper fans," she says. Pilot Polly starts to fan the crew with cool air.

"Aaaahhhhh!" says Mike, "that's lovely."

The crew are feeling much cooler and they all decide to buy a fan to take home with them.

Back on the plane, the cabin crew do their checks and Pilot Polly programmes the plane's computers.

Pilot Polly decides how much fuel she needs for the journey and the Spanish engineer fills up the plane's wings.

Soon the passengers arrive, but there is a problem! Everyone arrives at the same time and there is a big queue to get on to the plane.

The passengers are getting hot in the blazing sunshine. Luckily the crew have their fans and they pass them out so the passengers can fan themselves and cool down.

Eventually everyone is on board and in their seats. Megan closes the plane's huge door.

Pilot Polly speaks on her radio to the controllers in Madrid then starts the big jet engines.

She shouts "**Chocks Away!**" and taxies the plane to the runway for takeoff.

The jet engines go **ROOOOOAAAAARR!!** as Pilot Polly increases the power for takeoff.

The plane goes faster and faster and faster until it lifts up into the sunny sky.

Pilot Polly reaches forward and lifts the lever to put the wheels up and they set off back to London.